NUTS ABOUT NUTS

Diane Wilmer

Illustrated by Paul Dowling

FOREST HOUSE

REINFORCED LIBRARY BINDING

This is the story of Mr. Conker
who doesn't like winter,
doesn't like spring,
doesn't even like summer,
but he *loves* fall.

You might think he loves fall
because of the cool weather and
leaves changing color.
Oh no!
Mr. Conker loves fall for one thing only…

NUTS, especially horse chestnuts.
He is, quite simply, stark raving
NUTS ABOUT NUTS!

Down at the edge of Mr. Conker's yard
there's an enormous horse chestnut tree.
It's grown from a nut his great-grandfather
planted one hundred and fifty years ago.

It's never been cut, pruned, or trimmed,
and every year it's taller and thicker
than the year before.

In the springtime when the tree
starts to shed its buds,
Mr. Conker is on the lookout for
teeny-tiny horse chestnuts.

He takes his lawn chair out into
the yard and sits staring up at
the baby chestnuts growing in the sunshine.
"Conker is bonkers," yell the kids.
"Conker is bonkers," whisper the neighbors.
Mr. Conker doesn't care.
Every day, all summer long, he sits
and watches and waits.

Then one fall morning when Mr. Conker is
out in his yard, snoozing under the
tree—BONK!
Something falls on his head.
"OUCH!" yells Mr. Conker.

Lying in his lap is a horse chestnut,
the first one to fall, and it's still
in its prickly green case.

Mr. Conker squeezes it and out pops the horse chestnut.
Smooth, brown, big and round.

"YIPPEE!" he shouts, and waits all
day for more to fall. But not one of them does.

They just hang there, fat and heavy
on the tree, waiting for the right moment.

As the days grow shorter and cooler,
the horse chestnuts begin to lose their hold
on the branches. They rattle and bounce
all over the yard. But Mr. Conker always
finds them and he keeps every single one.

Now, when he sits in the yard, he wears a
motorcycle helmet and holds a bucket
between his knees.

"Come and get me, you beauties!" he roars
as he whacks the tree with his rake.
The chestnuts shower down like raindrops.
CLUNK…PING…BONG…BONK!

Mr. Conker laughs out loud as the nuts
bounce off his helmet and rattle into his bucket.
"Conker is bonkers!" yell the kids.
"Conker is bonkers!" whisper the neighbors.
But Mr. Conker doesn't care.

As the fall days pass, fewer and
fewer chestnuts fall from the old
tree. But my goodness, you
should see the inside of Mr. Conker's house!
He's got them in boxes, bags, buckets,
and barrels.

They're piled up on the television,
lined along the window sills,
mounded onto shelves,
dotted around the carpet,
and pouring out of the basement.

As fall comes to a chilly end, there's
only one chestnut left at the top of the tree.
The biggest, fattest, smoothest, brownest horse chestnut
of them all!

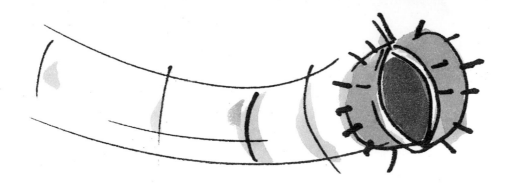

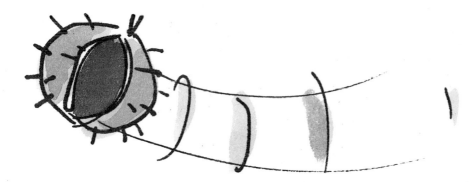

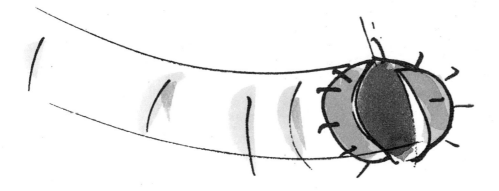

It hangs there, ripe and heavy.
Swinging back and forth…
back and forth…day…after…
day…after…day!

Mr. Conker thinks that chestnut will drive him bonkers!

He wants it more than he's ever wanted anything, but he can't get at it!

He tries whacking the tree trunk with the rake, but it doesn't work this time.

He tries shaking the tree with his bare hands.
"GRRRRRR!" That doesn't work either.

He tries climbing up, but it is too high.

He tries blowing it down.
"PHEWWW!"
But that's useless.

He tries jumping up and down and shouting at it.
"Come down here, you great, big, fat thing!"
That certainly doesn't work.

"Conker is bonkers!" yell the kids.

"Conker is bonkers!" whisper the neighbors.
"I DON'T CARE!" shrieks Mr. Conker.
"I just want THAT nut."

And he hits the tree with his big boot.

The nut wobbles
and shakes…
Tumbles and bumps
slowly
through
the leafy

branches
and lands
at his
feet.

BONK!

It's beautiful.
Mr. Conker puts it in his pocket.
Then he runs inside
and comes rushing out
with all his bags, buckets,
barrels and boxes of horse chestnuts.

"Here!" he yells to the kids.
"Have these."
"But...what about you?" they ask.

Mr. Conker just smiles and holds out the last chestnut.
"I'm all right," he says. "I've got this one.
The biggest and the best of them all."

This edition first published in the United States in 1990 by Gallery Books, an imprint of W.H. Smith Publishers, Inc. First published in the United Kingdom in 1989 by William Collins Sons and Co. Ltd. Produced for Gallery Books by Joshua Morris Publishing, Inc. in association with William Collins Sons and Co. Ltd. Text copyright © 1989 by Diane Wilmer. Illustrations copyright © 1989 by Paul Dowling. All rights reserved. ISBN 0-8317-4456-1. Printed in Hong Kong.